To schedule a school visit or inquire about related events, please contact by email at info@inbloompress.com.

In Bloom Press
Based out of Redding, California.

Thank you to Brooke Vitale, for her help editing this piece.

Published by In Bloom Press. Printed in the United States of America.

Paperback ISBN: 978-1-957016-00-9

Oh, Dear! Height is my Fear!

Written by Effie May
Illustrated by Terri Einer

In Bloom Press

Dedication

Special thank you to my family,
Dad, Mom, Jamie, and Chase,
for graciously supporting me over the years,
including with my own fears

Howdy, my name is Q! I am an acorn.

Right now, I'm stuck on my mama's branch.

Okay, okay . . .

Truth is, I'm hanging on for dear life!

Mama says I can't stay on her branch forever.

If I want to grow up big and tall like her, I have to drop. I need the soil to plant, sprout, and grow.

The growing part sounds good to me. It's the *falling* part I have a problem with.

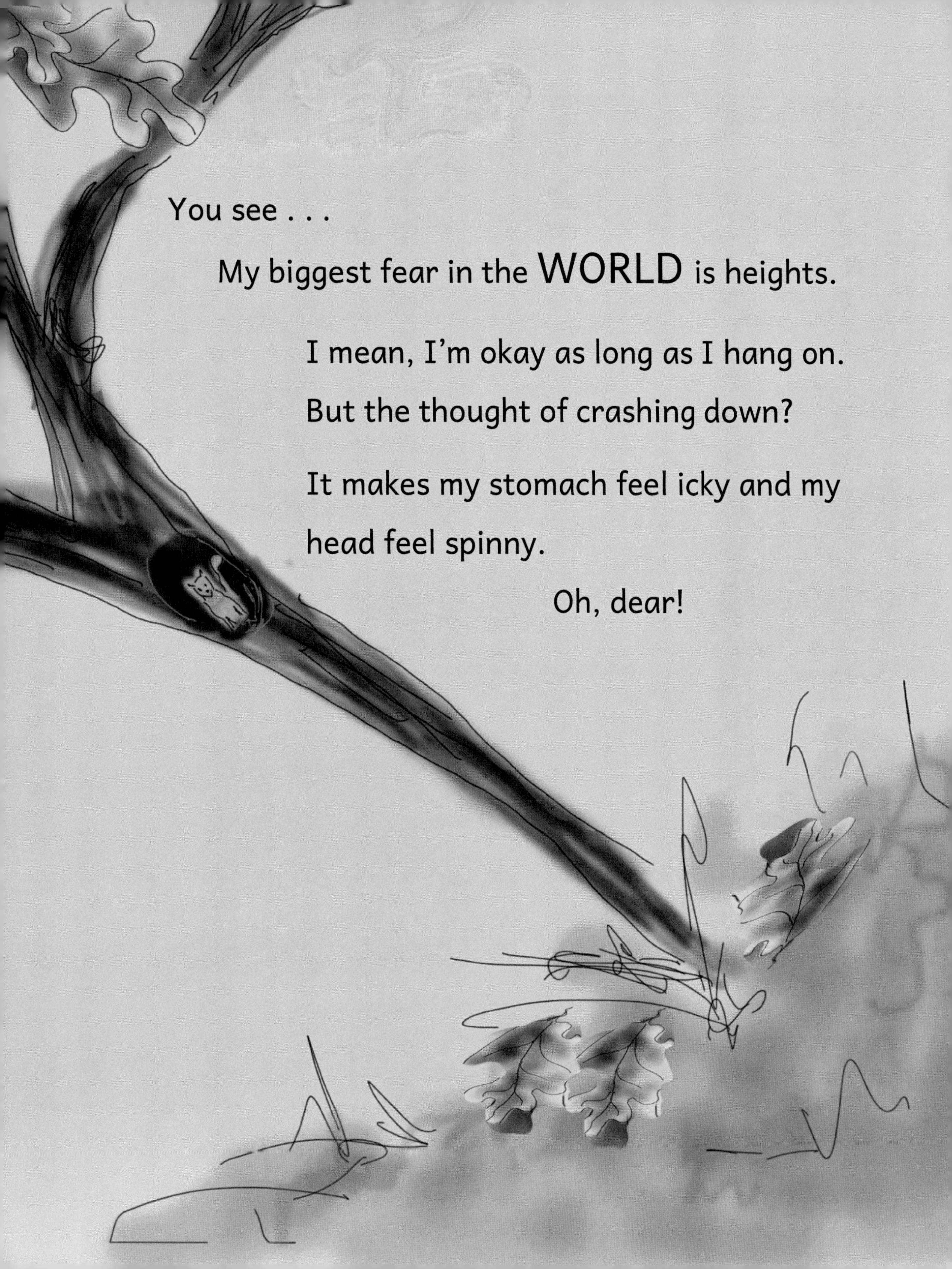

You see . . .

My biggest fear in the WORLD is heights.

I mean, I'm okay as long as I hang on.

But the thought of crashing down?

It makes my stomach feel icky and my head feel spinny.

Oh, dear!

This branch *used* to be fun.
All day long, I'd hang out with my
brothers and sisters.

But one by one, they all took the plunge.

Some jumped, others fell.

Some screamed . . . a lot.

One sister yelled,

"COWABUNGA!"

and leapt like a cannonball!

Let me tell you, they were the brave ones.

I wish I could be brave like them.

But I’m not. I’m scared.

What will happen once I fall?

I don’t even know what happened to everyone else.

Are they okay?

Do they miss me, too?

My heart is beating fast when Lady the Bug flies by.

"Hey, Q!" she buzzes. "Where is everyone?"

"They dropped! Mama says all acorns have to."

"Then why are you still here?" Lady asks.

"I'm too scared to branch out," I admit.
"When I think of dropping, I shake and shiver.
The fall must be hundreds and hundreds, or
even *thousands* of inches! What if I get hurt?"

"Did the other acorns get hurt?" Lady asks.

"I don't know! I haven't heard a peep since they dropped."

"Oooh, that **is** scary," Lady agrees. "You said all acorns have to drop, so they must be okay! What happens if you don't drop?"

I whimper, then I whisper.

“I won’t grow into a big, tall tree like my Mama. I need the soil to grow, and the soil is all the way down there.”

I steal the tiniest peek over my plump acorn belly down to the ground.

My ears and eyes are wide open.

I wish I knew if my brothers and sisters were okay.

Then . . . I hear it.

What's that sound?

Where are you, Q?

Q!

Q! We miss you!

That’s my name!

My brothers and sisters are calling my name!

They want me to join them!

Hearing their voices,
my fear starts to shrink.

I even smile a little.

Come play with us, Q!

Hey, Q!

"Go, Q!" Lady cheers.

"Think of it as flying, not falling!"

I start to let go, then stop.

"What is it like to fly?" I ask.

Lady smiles. "It is the best feeling in the world!"

I nod and look down again.

Flying. The best feeling in the world.

Down below, my brothers and sisters are

waiting for me.

I take a deep breath.

“Lady, will you count to 3? On 3, I’ll drop.”

I squeeze my eyes tight and Lady counts.

“1, 2, 3!”

But I don't drop. I just can't do it.

Far below, I hear my family cheering.

"You can do it, Q!"

SNAP!

Uh-oh!

Lady counts again. “1 . . . 2 . . . ”

SNAP!

My branch snaps before Lady says 3!

I yelp for help and cover my eyes!

I fall faster and FASTER!

I think I’m going to be sick!

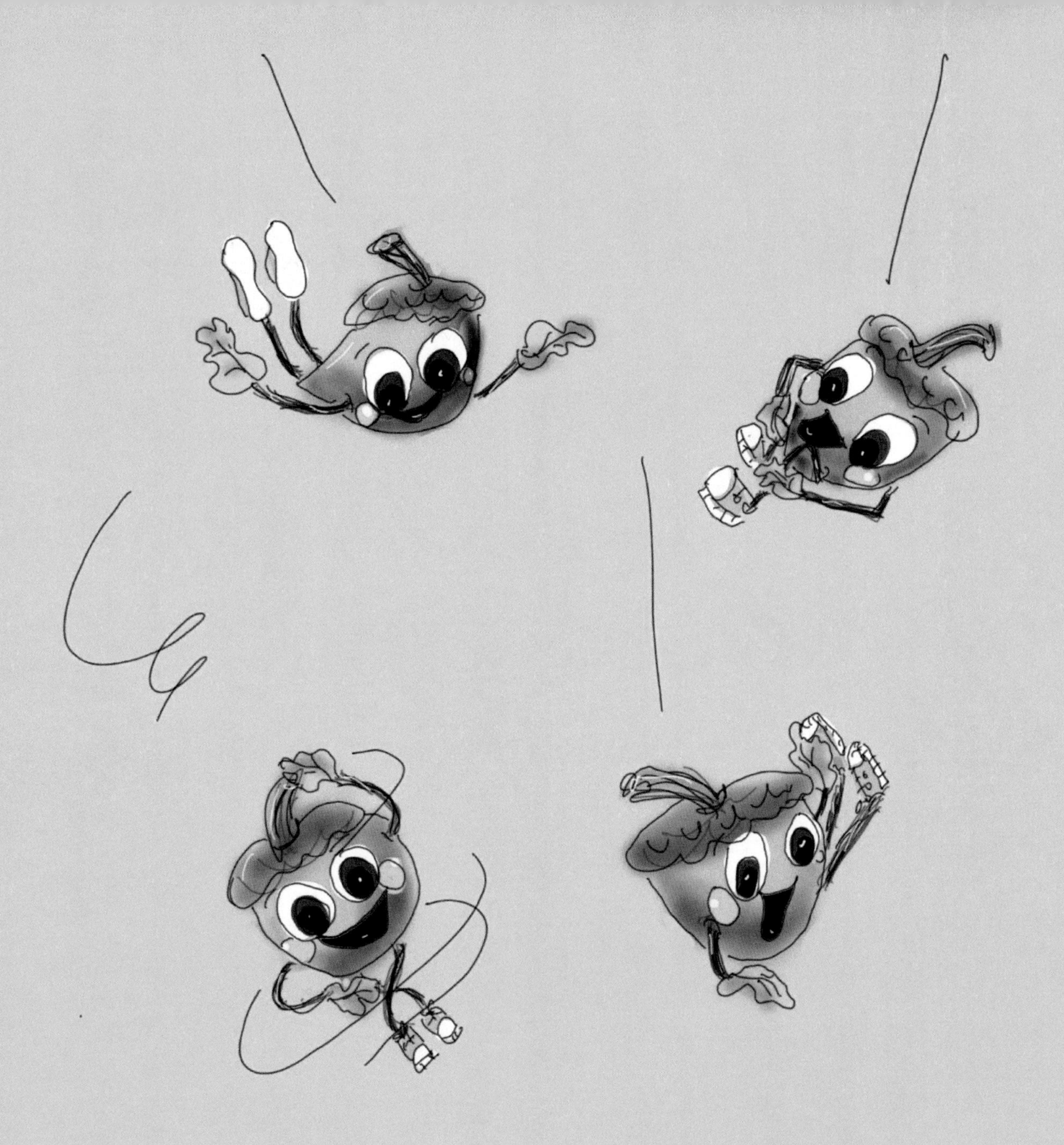

Wait . . . This drop is kind of fun!

I can twist and shout. I can strike a pose.

And I can tuck into a cannonball!

Then . . . *WHAM!*

I hit the dirt really, *really* hard.

It hurt. A lot.

Close by, I hear my brothers
and sisters gasp in shock.

I stand and I brush myself off.
I look at my feet and my hands.
I touch my head . . .

Then I shout. "That . . . was . . . AWESOME!"

Around me, everyone cheers and we jump into one big bear hug.

For the first time, I feel brave and tough.

I did it! I beat my biggest fear!

Maybe I didn't drop on purpose, but I did drop.

And it wasn't so scary!

"Woo-hoo!" I hoot.

"Woo-hoo!" We all hoot together.

I'm back with my family, and it feels great!

I'm so glad that I had to branch out!

Five Fun Facts About Oaks

Scientists make up names for all living things, called "scientific names."
They call oak trees Quercus. That's what Q is named after!

How tall can oak trees grow?
Up to 100 feet tall! That's a big drop for poor acorns like Q!

How many acorns can a huge oak tree (like Q's Mama) make every year? Some of the biggest oaks drop 10,000 acorns a year! That's a LOT of brothers and sisters!

Oak trees can live for a long time.
Many live to be over 300 years old!

Acorns usually drop from oak trees in autumn.
Autumn is a great time for seeds to plant because they can soak up the winter rain!

Author Effie May wrote her first books in kindergarten, and has loved storytelling ever since. A former environmental educator, she traded in campfire stories for picture books. For her free nature art activity, visit the following website: effiemay.ck.page

If you enjoyed meeting Q, please consider leaving a review!

Illustrator Terri Einer's quirky, loose style has lent itself to several picture books. Working out of her Oshkosh, WI studio, she loves bringing the author's words to life. You can contact the artist by visiting her website: www.terrieiner.com

Made in the USA
Las Vegas, NV
29 October 2021